For Cats' Eyes Only

Top secret book

only to be opened by

_____

Other titles by Olli Tooley

Time Tunnel series
- Time Tunnel to Londinium
- Londinium Revisited
- Time Tunnel at the Seaside
- Time Tunnel to West Leighton
- Time Tunnel to Ironbridge

Wise Oak series (Oliver J Tooley)
- Children of the Wise Oak
- Women of the Wise Oak

For Cats' Eyes Only

by
Olli Tooley
Illustrated by
Amii James
In association with
Ilfracombe Library
and
David Tubby
Published by

BLUE POPPY PUBLISHING

I would like to thank everyone in 6MN Ilfracombe Junior School 2017.

Aaron	Georgia-Rose
Alex	Grace
Alicia	Harvey
Amber	Jack
Bella	James
Chloe	Katie-Marie
Daisy	Leah
Dolores	Lulu
Dylan H.	Phoebe
Dylan L.	Ronnie
Ellie Marie	Rosie
Ellie-Rose	Ruby
Emily	Tahlia
Gemma	And Mr Newell

Prologue
The End ... Or is it?

"Not one more step, Swifty!"

Special Agent Felix Whiter sighted down the barrel of his Buckthorn and Beech .22 pistol at the tortoise, who had thought he was getting away. Swifty knew he could hide in his shell but, either way, there was no escape this time.

"Felix! I wish I could say I've been expecting you but, alas, it seems you have the upper hand."

"Did you really think you could get

away with it, Swifty?"

"Well, I guess I didn't expect that you would be assigned to the investigation. You're a cool cat, I'll give you that."

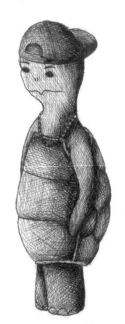

"My team are already rounding up your minions, and the lettuces are safely back in our warehouse. Now I just have to bring you in to make this a purrfect day."

As the secret agent spoke, Swifty looked past him with a worried expression.

"I'm not falling for that old trick, Swifty. There's nothing behind me."

"Wanna bet?"

Felix swung round and sure enough, a little girl was coming towards them across the grass. She must have seen everything. Desperately he tried to hide the gun behind his back and dropped down onto all fours, purring and flicking his tail, but it was no use. He'd been caught.

The little girl looked at the cat, and then at the tortoise which was trying to look innocent and slowly sidling away towards a large oak stump.

"Did I just see you talking to that tortoise, puss-cat?" the little girl asked.

"Meow?"

"It's no use pretending, I know I saw you standing up and pointing a stick at the tortoise, and you're wearing clothes, and you were definitely talking, although I didn't hear what you were saying."

"Purr?"

Felix stalked over to the little girl and rubbed hard against her legs with his sides, purring and meowing for all he was worth.

'Just a few minutes of this and she's

going to forget all about it,' thought Felix.

Sure enough, the girl began to doubt herself. "I must have imagined it," she said to herself as she scratched behind the cat's ears. "I suppose some people do like to dress their cats in clothes as well," she added.

At that moment, the cat turned its head to look at the point where the tortoise had been, only moments before. It was nowhere to be seen.

'Drat!' Felix thought.

Chapter 1

Bunny You Should Say That

The girl stood up and said, "Well pussycat, I have to be going now."

She wandered back in the direction she had come from. There seemed to be a lone human house. Some sort of farm, Felix assumed. It was on the edge of the woods, and beyond that was Wilder Moor. Humans generally meant trouble and Felix kept well away from them if he could. He approached this house, though. A cute fluffy bunny rabbit hopped about in a fenced rabbit run in the garden.

When the girl was well out of earshot
he crept close enough to speak to it.

"Hi, I'm Felix."

The rabbit's nose wrinkled, whiskers

twitched, its eyes darted in the direction where the little girl had gone.

Eventually, it said,

"Hi, I'm Floppy."

"So, have you been here all this time?"

"Sure, where else would I be? In case you haven't noticed, I'm in a cage here."

"Yes, sorry, I don't know what I was thinking of. So, did you see which way the tortoise went?"

"My memory is a little shaky sometimes."

"It was just a few minutes ago!"

"Yeah well, I got this funny memory. Things seem to come flooding back whenever I see money!"

"Oh. I see. Well here's a fifty-leaf note, can you see that?" Felix held the note up a little way from the wire mesh of the cage.

"Sorry, did I say when I can see money? I meant when I've got the money in my paws."

"What use is money to you anyway? You get all the lettuces and carrots you need, don't you?"

"Oh, so you think just because I'm a pet I don't have any ambition huh? Typical cat, only thinking of yourself."

"Here, take the money. Now tell me where the tortoise went."

"Sure. A little trap door opened up in that old oak tree stump. The tortoise disappeared down there. Have a nice day mister.

Chapter 2

Couldn't Give a Hoot

Felix returned to the Animal Intelligence Service headquarters, at Beech House. He pressed a buzzer and the face of an owl appeared on the intercom screen.

"Whoo is it?"

"Special Agent Felix Whiter."

"He's not here."

"It's me Olli. I'm Felix."

"Felix who?"

"Special Agent Felix Whiter."

"He's not here right now."

Felix began to get a little irritated, but he calmly tried again, "Olli, let me in, I'm here to see M!"

"Whoo shall I say is calling?"

"Special Agent Felix Whiter."

"He's not here right now."

Felix took a deep breath, closed his eyes, and counted to ten.

When he looked at the screen again there were the familiar white face and antlers of Jonathan Hart, M's assistant.

'Thank goodness for that,' thought Felix.

Chapter 3
Squeak and You Shall Find

Felix took the lift to the seventh floor and stepped out into the wood-panelled corridor. He knocked on the big door at the end and entered the office of his boss, the head of A.I.S.

It was a large and luxurious office. A polished walnut desk held an ink-well, a blotter and a notepad. The big black leather chair was empty. Someone was counting, and a repetitive squeaking sound came from somewhere out of sight. Felix walked around the desk to where the noise was coming from. A white mouse was running furiously around inside a wheel.

"Ninety-three, ninety-four … be with you … ninety-five … shortly … ninety-six … Felix … ninety-seven … ninety-eight … ninety-nine … … one hundred!"

Puffing and panting, the white mouse clambered out of the wheel, grabbed a big fluffy white towel from the antlers of the white stag waiting patiently nearby and began to wipe the sweat from her brow.

She grabbed a water bottle from a side table and ran up a ramp to the big black leather office chair.

She turned to the stag. "Be a deer and bring us two coffees, would you?"

She turned back to Felix. "Take a seat, Felix." She gestured to the smaller chair opposite, and Felix sat with his legs curled up on the chair.

M went on, "So how did the great lettuce heist case go? Got your tortoise, I presume?"

"He got away at the last minute."

"Oh, Felix! How could you let him escape?"

"Swifty by name, swift by nature, M.

That tortoise is a slippery customer. Besides, I was interrupted by a little girl."

"A girl? Well, I hope she didn't see anything ... untoward."

"I smoothed everything over, but that's when Swifty gave me the slip. But I'll track him down, mark my words."

"Never mind Swifty now, Felix. A much more serious problem has come up; I need you to get onto it right away."

"But ..."

"No buts, in fact, that's sort of the problem."

"Go on, M."

"The General's baby goat, Billie, has gone missing. We think she's been ... kid-nabbed."

"Oh gosh."

"Yes, gosh, indeed. He loves that little goat as though she is his own daughter."

"Has there been a ransom note?"

"Not yet, but I want you to start poking around and see what you can find out. The kid was hanging around at the 'Juice Bar' over on Hedge Row. A lot of the customers are dogs, it's pretty rough, but you might pick up a few leads."

"I think I can handle myself. Just worried about the poor kid. Why would she go somewhere like that?"

"You know how some people are. Always complaining about being nannied? Anyway, off you go Felix, and see what you can turn up."

Felix hesitated and thought for a moment, then said, "My collar?"

"What?"

"I can turn up my collar, M."

M looked irritated. "I was talking about in your investigations."

"Oh, that. Right. I'll be off then."

As Felix opened the door, M added, "Oh; pop in on Sydnee before you go. He might have something useful for you."

Chapter 4
The Worldwide Web

Sydnee's office was back down the corridor. Felix knocked. From the other side, there was a muffled voice.

"Just a minute! ... Argh! Get back you ..."

It sounded as though Sydnee was in serious trouble; Felix tried the handle without success. Then he gave the door an almighty push. With a splintering sound, the door burst open and Felix half charged, half fell into the small office where a spider, wearing glasses, was sitting in front of a computer screen. He turned.

"What have you done to my door, you moggie maniac?"

"Oh, sorry Sydnee, I thought there was someone attacking you." Felix looked at the computer screen. It read,

Sydnee had the decency to look embarrassed as he clicked 'N' and opened up a different program on the computer.

"We got CCTV images from just outside the Juice Bar. Billie-the-Kid was seen talking to a Staffordshire bull terrier just before she disappeared. We ran his mugshot through our database on the worldwide web. His name's Dudley, and it turns out he's got a record."

"Really? I usually just use MP3s nowadays. Takes up less space."

"I was talking about his criminal record."

"What, like Ellie Gelding or Justin Beaver's greatest hits?"

"No, I mean like petty theft, aiding and abetting, that sort of thing."

"Oh, yes, of course. I knew what you meant. I was just …"

"Yes, well, anyway, here's a recent photograph of Dudley. Best of luck Felix."

Chapter 5

It's a Dog's Life

Felix walked along Hedge Row. Everywhere he looked there were new young plants sprouting up; a sure sign this was a seedy part of town. The Juice Bar was up ahead on a corner. As he went in, the hubbub of noise suddenly turned to a deathly silence, and Felix found himself looking down the muzzle of a Rottweiler.

"What's a nice little cat like you doing in a dog bar, huh?"

"I'm looking for someone, but you're not him, so you'd best just move aside, buddy."

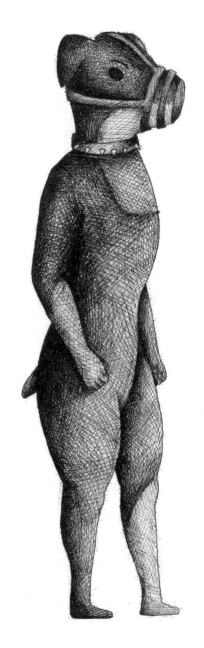

24

"Hey, how'd you know my name?"

"Just a lucky guess. What do folks drink in here anyway?" Felix asked casually.

"Mostly milk and fruit juice. Ice cream, and lollies for those who like the harder stuff."

Several other dogs were moving closer.

Buddy leered at Felix. "Anyway, who do you think you are coming in here and telling me what to do?"

Felix stretched his claws out nonchalantly. He flashed his I.D. card and said, "Special Agent, Felix Whiter. Who am I? I'm your worst nightmare, Buddy. I'm a moggie with a badge."

At that moment the other dogs, having surrounded Felix, all charged at him from different directions. Faster than the eye, Felix leapt upwards, leaving the dogs to crash into each other, snarling and biting. Felix landed and slashed claws into all four dogs at once, sending them howling to the corners of the room. Only Buddy remained, his nose dripping blood.

"OK, Mr Special Agent, you made your point. So what can I do for you?"

"I'm looking for a Staffy; goes by the name of Dudley."

Felix showed the photograph to Buddy the Rottweiler.

"He comes in here sometimes, was in yesterday."

"Anyone know where he lives?" Felix said to the room in general.

Everyone in the place seemed to be paying very close attention to their drinks.

Felix took a deep breath and said loudly and clearly, "I reckon I could have fifty uniformed police down here in ten minutes, and we'd find something on everyone in this joint."

He strolled past some of the dogs, cowering at a table.

"A few more worming tablets than maybe one dog needs?"

A group of foxes were sitting at the next table.

"Maybe somebody's visa might have run out?"

A lone wolf skulked in a corner.

"Maybe we search someone's pad, and find a mob-cap and nightdress linked to a missing granny?"

He turned slowly, looking around the room.

"Even if you stinking low-lifes haven't done anything, are you sure I won't put something there to find?"

There was a faint whining from one young pup.

"But hey!" Felix smiled a radiant smile, "Who needs all that paperwork? Not me. I just want to find one dog and ask him some questions. Is that so hard?"

Chapter 6

Chairman of the Boar-d

At the very back of the bar a door opened. A boar, almost as wide as the doorway, waddled through.

"What's all dis? Buddy, who is this guy?"

"Ah, sorry boss, he's some special agent wants to talk to one o' the regular customers, boss."

The boar stared intensely at the white cat in the impeccable suit.

"Why don't you step into my office and we can have a civilised chat Mr...?"

"Whiter, Felix Whiter, licenced to chill. And you are?"

"Don Ramon Serrano, at your service, Mr Whiter."

They entered his office. It was oak-panelled, with red leather wing chairs. The desk was ornate, with gold handles, and decorative beading. Behind the desk was a painting, in a gilt frame. It showed a grand looking boar wearing the clothes of a hundred years ago.

Don Serrano saw Felix looking at the painting.

"My great grandfather, Giuseppe Serrano."

Felix sought for something nice to say.

"He looks very dashing."

"So what brings you to my humble establishment Mr Whiter? I run a respectable business here, so you got no need to come in here beatin' up the customers, you know what I'm sayin'?"

"Maybe you should tell your customers to treat cats with a little more respect then. Besides, all I want is to talk to a dog named Dudley."

"Never heard of him."

"Oh really, well I have information that he did a few odd jobs for you, a year or two back. Ended up in the pound."

"Nothin' to do with me, I told ya, I run a clean operation here. Strictly legit."

"Fine, well, you won't mind if the

uniform boys go over this place then. You know, they just won't stop gnawing until they have stripped a place clean. Even if you're legit like you say, some of your customers might not be. Could be bad for business if the guys propping up your bar end up behind a five bar gate with nothing but oats in their trough."

"OK, maybe I do know this Dudley, an' maybe I give ya his address. I don't wanna see your ugly feline mug round here again, we got a deal?"

"Oh, we have a deal alright. Nothing will give me greater pleasure."

Chapter 7

Something Stinks

Dudley's pad was in a part of town known as the 'Bone Yard'. It was a flea bitten, run down area, but Felix wasn't afraid. That's more than could be said for Dudley. He seemed alright when he first opened the door, but then Felix spoke.

"Hello, I'm Special Agent Felix Whiter of A.I.S." He flashed his I.D. card.

At that moment Dudley became obviously nervous. His Black Country accent was so thick you could slice it with a knife.

"Y' alright, err … what do you want

then, like?"

"A kid went missing last night. You were the last known person to see her."

"It wasn't me; I never done nothing!"

There was a very quiet 'pfft' sound, un-noticed by Felix.

"I need to ask you about your movements between ... what is that smell?"

"Yer makin' me nervous! An' when I get nervous, I sort of ... tend to ... you know?"

"Shoot the breeze? Float air biscuits?"

"I was gonna say 'guff' but, yeah, that."

"Have you considered dry feed? That's revolting. It smells like something died."

"Sorry!"

Dudley wafted his paw to wave away the smell, muttering under his breath, "Oi quite like it actually."

"Good grief, dog. I was going to suggest we discuss this inside, but maybe a walk around the yard might be preferable."

They walked to the small yard area, with Dudley clearly very nervous the whole time, judging by the number of little puffs of vile smelling gas that he produced every now and then.

"So you admit you saw Billie-the-Kid last night?"

"Yes, but oi didn't do nothin'." Pfft.

Felix gagged as he walked faster to get away from the smell. "So where did she go after she was with you?"

"She said she was headed home. She lives in a really posh part o' town, so I thought she'd be safe." Pfft.

Felix pulled a hankie from his pocket and put it over his nose and mouth.

"So which way was she headed when she left?"

She was headed towards Beech Avenue is all I know." Pfft.

Felix's eyes were streaming now.

"Thank you, Dudley, you've been most helpful."

"I hope she's not hurt. She's a good kid that Billie. I wouldn't want any harm to come to her, like." Pfft.

It was with considerable relief that Felix left the yard and headed back towards headquarters.

Chapter 8
The Wilder Moor Beast

Back at H.Q. the information Felix had gained took second place to a ransom note.

If you want to see Billie-the-Kid alive ever again, bring Ł1,000,000 to the blasted oak on Wilder Moor

sincerely,

the Wilder Moor Beast

"A million leaves! Wow, who's got that kind of money?" asked Felix.

"The General has," was M's reply. "But he's not happy about this. He wants that kid back safe, but he doesn't want to be seen to give in to hostage takers. There'd be no end to it."

"What do you propose we do?"

"You'll have to go undercover."

"What, you mean, like, put a blanket over my head?"

"No, you crazy cat, I'm talking about deep cover."

"I'm usually a bowler, or silly-mid-off."

"I'm not talking about cricket! I mean you will have to have a disguise."

"Oh! A disguise! Of course. Good plan M."

The mouse pressed the intercom, "Jonathan, would you send Carla in please?"

The white stag opened a door and ushered in a pretty chameleon.

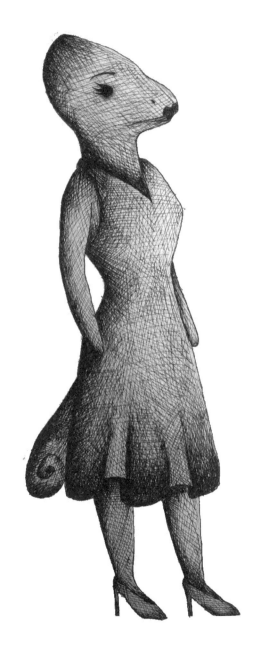

"Carla, this is Felix; he needs to go undercover. What have you got?"

"Perfect," Carla enthused, "We've just developed a sophisticated prosthetic badger costume. Mechanical digging claws, night vision goggles, the works. This will be the ideal test for it."

Felix adjusted his tie and smoothed back his fur. He leant forwards in his chair, and looked deep into Carla's great big chameleon eyes.

"I have pretty good night vision already."

Carla went on, "Not like this. I think you'll be impressed by what you see."

"I'm already impressed by what I see," he said, leaning forward still further until he was quite close to Carla. Then he slipped and fell off his chair.

Carla stood up.

"Come to our labs for a fitting in half an hour," she said, as she left the office.

Felix stood up and tried to look cool. M looked at him, shaking her head, and said, "Pop in and see Sydnee on your way over, Felix."

Chapter 9

A Mine of Information

Sydnee was busy trying to locate a series of land-mines on the computer screen when Felix entered. Felix kept quiet, as it seemed like a tense moment. As far as he could make out, Sydnee was locating these mines remotely, and he wondered where the actual mines were located, and what would happen if he detonated one. He had already located thirty-five mines and was trying to decide if one last one was in the corner of the screen or next to it. Sweat pouring off his brow, Sydnee finally took the plunge and clicked a square. The mine exploded, as did all the others on the screen. Felix finally spoke.

"Oh dear!"

Sydnee had not realised Felix was there and he jumped right out of his seat and landed in a corner of the ceiling. Lowering himself back down he looked rather upset.

"What did you go and do that for? You nearly scared the living daylights out of me."

"Sorry, Sydnee. Will there be many casualties from those mines going off?"

"Oh, that. Err, no, it was just an exercise, this time."

"Oh, thank goodness for that," Felix said.

"Yes. I'm glad you popped in Felix. Here, we've developed a new hi-tech gadget for you to try out. Wireless fungal network connection headset. Wi-Fu for short. Anywhere there's a mushroom, you are connected automatically. In-ear monitor; allows you to hear instructions from H.Q. Tiny eye camera, here; so that what you see, we see."

Felix put the headset on.

"Feels unobtrusive. Where are the controls?"

"Volume here, spy-cam on-off switch here. We like to keep it simple for field agents."

Felix fiddled with the controls.

"What's this button?"

"Oh, a little extra thing we added. That just releases a waft of scent; saves time if you have to go to a posh party and you want to smell nice."

"Nice touch."

Felix always liked to smell good. He pressed the button and there was a 'pfft' sound, followed by a fragrant waft of musk.

"Mm, Camel No. 5, my favourite."

Sydnee went on, "Now, we've found something out about the so-called 'Wilder Moor Beast'. The ransom note was printed using the local library printer."

"So you're saying we are dealing with a criminal mastermind then?"

"What?"

"He's one smart cookie this 'Wilder Moor Beast'."

"What are you talking about Felix?"

"Well, printing at the library is good value for money."

"Oh that. Yes, but I only meant that you could start by checking out anyone who has a library card."

"Oh, yes, good idea Sydnee. I'll do that."

Chapter 10

Throw the Book at Him

The badger suit was a perfect disguise. Felix found he could mingle with close friends unrecognised, and blend in with forest animals without causing suspicion.

He tried it out, popping down to the local library. The librarian was an attractive sow by the name of Cathy. She knew Felix well, but with his badger disguise, she didn't recognise him at all. When he tried to borrow a book using his own library card she immediately got suspicious.

"Snort; I'm sorry sir but this isn't your card," she told him sternly.

"What?"

Felix had actually forgotten he was wearing the disguise.

"I happen to know this is Felix Whiter's card and he's a regular customer here."

"It's me, Cathy. Felix."

He lifted the mask of the badger suit.

"Felix! Squee!"

"Shh, not so loud," he hissed.

Cathy snuffled, "Sorry are you working undercover?"

"Well, yes, that too, but I meant, not so loud, this is a library!"

"Oh, yes, good point. I sometimes forget." She suppressed a giggle, "Snortle-snort."

"I need some information," Felix whispered.

"Of course; you know where the reference section is."

"This is information on your

customers."

"Oh, right, yes of course. What do you need to know?"

"Has anyone used the printers recently?"

"We get about a hundred people a day using the printers, Felix."

"Oh!" Felix looked crestfallen.

She went on, "And we have records of everything that gets printed off."

"So, would you be able to tell me who had this printed?" He showed her the ransom note.

"Let's take a look."

She sat at the desk and typed a few strokes on the keyboard. Within a moment she said, "Got it!"

"Brilliant!" said Felix. "How come the library are even better than the intelligence services at getting information?"

"We've had a lot of practice over the years."

"So who is this customer?"

"His name's Dudley. Do you want his address?"

"Let me guess. Number 4, The Kennels, Bone Yard?"

"Wow, how did you know?"

"Oh, just a lucky guess."

Felix looked dejected. He would have to go back to see the flatulent Dudley.

Chapter 11
It's an Ill Wind

Dudley was just walking back to his house when a badger jumped out from behind a tree.

"You startled me," the Staffy yelped. Pfft.

"Never mind that." Felix pressed the perfume release button. Pfft; a waft of Camel No.5 met the incoming cloud of Dudley's more unsavoury odour.

He grabbed Dudley by the collar and shoved him up against a wall. "You printed this ransom note. Don't try and deny it."

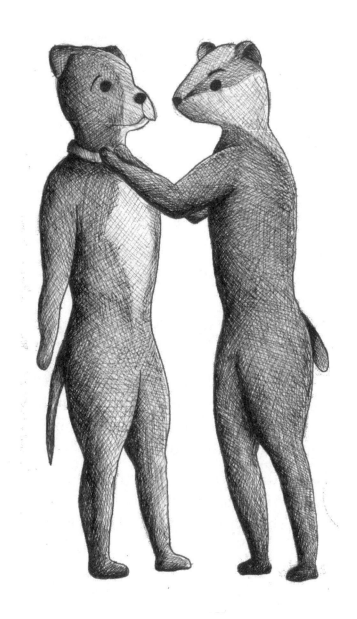

"Oi didn't want to. Oi was being blackmailed." Pfft.

"Did you write this note?"

"Write it? Oi can't even read!" Dudley wailed. "What does it say, anyway?"

Felix didn't tell him. He remembered that Dudley had said he really liked Billie-the-Kid, and he began to suspect he really meant it. Dudley was just a pawn in someone else's game.

"Who was blackmailing you?" Pfft.

Felix, inside the badger suit, thought to himself, 'I must remember to thank Sydnee for this headset.'

"It was that Don Ramon Serrano, from the 'Juice Bar'." Pfft. "Oi owe him a lot of money after oi got into trouble in a game of happy families. He said, if I did a little job for 'im, he would let me off."

"Oh, good grief." Pfft.

Felix put a ten-leaf note into Dudley's pocket.

"Thanks for the info Dudley. I'll see you around."

When the badger was a reasonable distance away Dudley muttered under his breath, "Not if I see you first."

Chapter 12

Play Your Cards Right

The badger strode confidently into the Juice Bar. Buddy the Rottweiler barely turned to look at him come in.

Badgers frequently came into town from the woods. They often had plenty of money when they arrived but by the time they had been to all the bars and gambling clubs in town they generally went home poorer but wiser.

The bartender was drying a glass with a cloth.

"What're you having?"

In a country accent, Felix said "Arr, milk."

"On the rocks?"

"Straight up."

The bartender poured a shot of milk into a glass.

"And leave the bottle," the badger said, placing a ten-leaf note on the bar.

The bartender took the note and continued wiping glasses with a cloth.

Felix took a long drink and then said, "Any high rollin' happy families games you know of?"

"That all depends on who's askin' and if they've got the leaves to hang out with the big boys."

Felix unfolded a small bundle of fifty-leaf notes and flicked through them, "How much is enough?"

The bartender's eyes opened wide, "That will do nicely," he said. Reaching under the bar, he pressed a button, and a door to the side slid open. The bartender indicated the door and said, "Go right on up. They'll be expecting you."

Felix finished his milk, picked up the bottle and sauntered casually through the door, which slid silently shut behind him.

He was in a corridor with deep plush carpets. Expensive paintings hung on the walls; Vincent Van-Frogh, Andy Warthog, Pablo Pigasso, Lion-ardo Da Vinci, Salvador Doggi; any one of them would cost more than Felix earned in a year.

He walked along the corridor to the only other door. He knocked and then entered. Seated around a table were several characters, each dressed in fine clothes.

At the head of the table was Don Ramon Serrano.

"I don't believe we've had the pleasure?"

Felix put on a country-bumpkin voice, "Arr, I'm Jethro Brock; just arrived in town."

"Pleased to make your acquaintance,"

the great boar said.

"Lemme introduce everyone here. This is Mickey the Duck." He indicated a big billy goat with an impressive goatee beard and an even more impressive quiff on top of his head.

Moving along the table, Don Serrano's eye reached a bull who filled his chair to bursting point. He had a ring through his nose, but against all common sense, he seemed quite timid, "This is Ferdie, the bull." Ferdie nodded, but failed to make proper eye contact.

Next along was a guinea-pig with a Mohican and a series of tattoos. He was introduced as Chiquito, and his eyes bored into Felix's as though he was trying to destroy him with a look.

Lastly, on the other side of the table, was a black rat with a scar across his right eye. He was introduced as Hans.

"We're just about to deal a new game." Serrano indicated the deck of cards. "Minimum stake fifty leaves, ten per family, one to buy, five to see. Ollie will change your money for chips."

Felix looked around, half expecting to see the stupid owl from headquarters. Instead, a very efficient octopus took his cash and distributed a stack of chips in various denominations.

Chapter 13

When the Chips are Down

The cards were dealt. Felix hadn't played happy families in a long while, but he had the assistance of Sydnee giving him instructions in his earpiece. Sydnee also fed him information on each of the characters around the table. None of them was completely clean, although few had actually been convicted of anything. They were all rich and could afford good lawyers. Felix wondered how it was that he worked really hard all year, and yet he wouldn't earn as much as some of these guys made in a single deal.

"Ask Hans for Miss Goat," came the advice over his headset from Sydnee.

"Hans, have you got Miss Goat?"

The rat gave the badger a look of sheer hatred and handed over the card. Now it was Hans' turn, and he asked Chiquito for Master Pig. Felix looked at Master Pig in his own hand and tried hard not to react.

"What about that kid-nabbing that was on the news?" the badger asked, by way of a conversation starter.

Nobody bit.

"Who do you suppose is this mystical 'Wilder Moor Beast', eh?"

Serrano spoke, "People who ask too many questions, often find out answers they don't want to hear."

Felix put on his most innocent face, "Ooh, do you know something then? I heard how it might be a boar. No offence."

"You ever hear the saying, 'careless talk costs lives'?" the boar asked.

"No, is that a townie thing then?"

"Could be."

As the game wore on, the stakes mounted up. There was enough money on the table for Felix to pay off his Barkley-card bill. Not that he would get to keep any of his winnings as he was gambling with agency money. He had a good hand now, but Serrano just raised the stakes even higher. Felix looked at his chips. He had barely enough to stay in the game. There was a tense moment. Back at H.Q. Sydnee had been joined by M.

"Stay in," Sydnee said, over the headset.

Felix slid his chips into the middle of the table.

"I'm out," Hans conceded.

The turn came back to Serrano, who raised the stakes yet again. Ferdie folded, Chiquito threw his cards across the table. As they flew, Sydnee captured the footage and rewound back through, checking which cards he'd had. Chiquito had the whole rat family, and most of the dogs, and mice. That meant that Felix must surely have the best hand.

"See him, Felix. You've got this."

Felix's mind was racing, he had no more cash on him. How could he stay in? He looked at his wrist. The gold Murex watch was worth a thousand leaves. It had been a present from his father, the late, great, Tiddles Whiter. He slipped it off his wrist and tossed it into the centre. "Let's see your cards then Don Serrano."

The great boar fanned his cards down on the table, "Two fours, two threes. My game I think?"

He reached forward to collect his winnings.

"Not so fast, Serrano," Felix laid his hand on the table with a flourish, "Three fours. Horses, cattle, and sheep. Read 'em and weep."

As Felix stretched out his badger paw to collect the chips, a seam came loose and his cat paw came out. Quickly he pulled it back in, but not before it had been spotted.

Chapter 14
The Game's Up

Felix was held fast by the powerful arms of the octopus. Chiquito had ripped his badger mask off and Serrano was holding an Oakzi sub-machine gun levelled at the cat's chest. It was a relief to Felix that the headset had come off with the mask and had not been spotted.

"Well, well, well. I thought we had a deal you wouldn't show your ugly puss anywhere near this joint, but here you are sneakin' around, cheatin' at cards."

"Not cheating, just better at the game. And at least I'm not a kid-nabber. I know it was you who sent that ransom note, demanding a million leaves for

Billie-The-Kid."

"Well done you, Mr Secret Agent. But alas, now you're gonna die; so the knowledge won't do you no good. Take him away Ollie."

Ollie dragged Felix through another door, and to an enormous fish-tank. Swimming around inside were several large and scary looking sharks. They looked hungry.

"Look, can't we talk about this?"

Serrano had followed them through to the tank.

"The time for talkin' is over. Now it's time for watchin' and dyin'. Me watchin', an' you dyin'."

"But aren't you going to reveal your entire devious plan before you kill me?"

"Nope. It ain't my plan anyways."

"What? Surely you're the evil mastermind behind all this?"

"Nope. That would be Mr Floppy."

"Mr Floppy?"

"Yeah, but he prefers to be known as the Wilder Moor Beast."

"So who is this Wilder Moor Beast then?" Felix hoped that the headset was still transmitting and that at least his death would not be in vain.

"No more questions moggie. Let's see how you can swim."

"Well, I got my bronze swimming certificate at school, so I'm pretty good actually."

"Did they have sharks in the pool when you took your test?"

"I thought you said no more questions! Hah! Got you."

"Oh sure; you got me alright. Ollie, throw him in the tank."

Felix sighed as he realised that he had won the argument but was about to lose his life.

Chapter 15

Panic Stations

Back at A.I.S. H.Q. it was complete panda-monium. Everyone was running around like headless chickens. M was giving out orders to anyone who stood still long enough to listen.

"Sydnee, get Glenn and 'Rubber' airborne, and heading over to the Juice Bar."

"Yes M."

Glenn was the eagle commander of the air force division. Bill 'Rubber' Duck was the naval commander.

"Get me Milly on Wi-Fu."

"Yes M."

Milly mole was the chief of the underground division.

"H.Q. to Milly; Are you reading me - over?"

"Reading you loud and clear; go ahead – over."

"Head over to the Juice Bar on Hedge Row. See if you can find a way in from underneath."

"Roger that – over."

"Felix is in big trouble. His cover's blown."

"Message received and understood. Out."

"Sydnee, send a message to 'Red' and get the arboreal guys on this, and tell Commander Timms to put every squad car he can spare on it as well."

That was Eric 'Red' Squirrel whose team operated among the trees, where Glenn Eagle's boys might have trouble seeing through the foliage, and Commander Timothy Timms, of the uniformed police, who were all rats.

"Oh, and get The General, he's going to want to be in on this."

The General was the great big boar who ruled over the animals with a firm but fair trotter. His enlightened reign had been long and prosperous and it was his baby goat who had been kid-nabbed.

With everyone converging on the Juice Bar, they would surely soon have Don Ramon Serrano locked up in the pen, along with Chiquito who was clearly dangerous and needed to be in a cage as soon as possible.

But would it be enough to save Felix?

Chapter 16
All for One

Hedge Row was filled with the sound of wailing sirens; ducks and eagles were swooping in overhead; moles were bursting out through the floorboards of the Juice Bar; rats were scurrying over every inch of the place. Customers were trying to climb out through windows or dashing for the fire escapes, but M's team had every escape covered and soon there were dozens of prisoners rounded up and hand-vined.

Ramon Serrano put up a fight but soon even he was well and truly tied up.

M brought Serrano before The General himself for questioning.

"So Serrano, we meet again."

They had both gone to school together. Serrano had been a bit of a bully then, but The General had driven himself hard, doing press-ups, and sit-ups, and going for long runs, until he could defend himself. He also worked harder in lessons and, as a result, had risen to become the leader of all the animals; and a popular leader he was too. Ramon, on the other hand, had been lazy at school and cheated in his exams, so although he was the big gangland boss, nobody really liked him.

"So what have you done with Billie-the-Kid?" asked The General.

"I wouldn't know. I never did no kid-nabbin'."

M spoke urgently, "Err, General? Felix?"

"Oh yes. Well, Serrano, we can discuss who kid-nabbed Billie later. First, we need to know where Felix is?"

"Him? He's swimmin' with da fishes."

"What do you mean?"

Serrano pointed, "Pull that lever and you'll see."

The General pulled the lever and a door slid open revealing the huge shark tank. The sharks were swimming around looking very contented. One of them opened its jaws and bubbles rose to the surface. When they burst, there was a loud burp.

"You evil pig! You threw Felix to the sharks?" M shouted.

"Yep."

Everyone looked really sad. Those wearing hats removed them and bowed their heads in honour of a much loved secret agent, and personal friend.

Behind them, a very wet white cat wearing the remains of a badger costume, also bowed his head to mourn whoever it was that had died.

Eventually, Olli the Owl, who was at the back of the room, noticed Felix. He burst into tears and hugged Felix.

"He was my best friend!" wailed Olli.

"Who was?" Felix asked.

"Why, Special Agent Felix Whiter of course! He's been eaten by sharks!"

"Has he?" Felix looked amused but puzzled.

"Wait, did you just get here?"

"Well, I was in deep water for a bit but I managed to drag myself away."

"So, who are you?"

Felix looked puzzled again.

"Special Agent Felix Whiter?"

Olli began wailing again, "He's been eaten by sharks!"

Jonathan Hart turned around to see what all the fuss was about.

"Felix!" he cried, grabbing Felix up and giving him a great big hug.

M turned round, "Aah, Felix, there you are. What kept you?"

"Well, I had to tangle with a malevolent octopus and escape from some really quite hungry sharks. But, it turns out sharks prefer calamari to cat. Who knew?"

Chapter 17

~~Mr Floppy~~ *The Wilder Moor Beast*

"Well, I'm glad you're safe," The General said, "Any leads on Billie?"

"Yes, General, I think I have an idea. M, have we got Glenn and Bill airborne?"

"Of course, Felix. I've got every animal we've got on the case."

"Right, well, have them fly over the farmhouse on the edge of the moor and check if there's a cute little bunny rabbit in a cage there, please."

When the report came back it was negative. Glenn had spotted the rabbit hutch and run, but there was no sign of the rabbit itself. He had even used heat sensitive camera goggles to double check the rabbit was not inside the hutch.

"Right, I need to get over there right away. Circulate this description of the 'Wilder Moor Beast' A.K.A. Mr Floppy Bunny. He's a honey coloured lop-eared rabbit. Looks cuter than a kitten in a onesie."

"Righto, you'd better have someone with you to watch your back," suggested M.

"OK, have Eric the Red keep an eye on things from the trees nearby. And get him to keep an eye on the old oak stump as well, while he's waiting."

"Right-oh, Felix. Good luck."

Chapter 18
A Few Nasty Surprises

Felix approached the farmstead where Mr Floppy normally resided. He was nowhere to be seen, which came as no surprise to Felix who had a theory about what was going on. He settled down behind a tuft of bracken to wait.

After a few minutes, Felix spotted movement in a corner of the rabbit run. A section of grass began to turn and then lifted up along with a thick layer of soil. The disc of turf was pushed aside and Mr Floppy emerged from the hole in the ground. He was wearing a long leather trench-coat, and sunglasses, which he now removed and placed into the tunnel. 'Talk about pretentious,' Felix thought to himself, 'wearing sunglasses in a tunnel.'

Felix waited until Mr Floppy had replaced the turf, before leaping the fence and into the run to confront the honey coloured lop. His Buckthorn and Beech .22 was cocked and at the ready.

"Not one twitch, Mr Floppy. Or should I say, Wilder Moor Beast?"

The bunny put his paws, and ears, in the air and turned slowly.

"Special Agent Felix Whiter. I've been expecting you."

Felix looked surprised.

"Really? Because, I'd have thought that if you were expecting me, you wouldn't have come back here, unarmed without any back-up."

"Who says I don't have back-up?"

Another disc of turf lifted up behind Felix. A fox emerged from the hole. Felix still had his pistol; he turned and moved closer to the hutch so that he could cover both fox and rabbit with one gun.

'I hope Red is working on a rescue plan,' thought Felix.

Suddenly, from on top of the hutch, a snake dropped down and knocked the gun spinning from his hand. Now Felix was outnumbered and unarmed. The snake wrapped itself around Felix, who slashed at it with his claws. The snake screamed and unwound, but then the fox leapt at him, knocking the wind out of his lungs. As he lay helpless on the floor, Mr Floppy leapt in and planted a series of fast kicks into his chest and head. The snake was now winding round his legs, preventing him kicking out or running away.

'Come on Red, where are you when I need you?'

The fox had Felix's arms behind his back now and Mr Floppy was punching him in the stomach. The sky began to go dark and there was a strange echoing to the sounds, as though everything was distant. Felix was vaguely aware that he was about to lose consciousness.

Chapter 19
The End ... Probably

Glenn swooped down and grabbed the snake in his talons. Bill 'Rubber' Duck landed in a flurry of down.

"Come at me foxy, let's see what you've got."

The fox turned to face his new challenger. He approached slowly, menacingly. As he got closer to 'Rubber' he was suddenly jumped by a huge and angry frog. It was James Pond, of the amphibious division, who had been carried in by Bill earlier, unnoticed by the villains who had been focussing all their attention on poor Felix.

Now all that remained was Mr Floppy himself. He was still slapping Felix about when suddenly a spider landed right on his face.

"Arrgh!" Mr Floppy yelled, "A spider! Get it off me!" he flailed around trying to flap the spider off his face without actually touching it; not a feat that anyone who was afraid of spiders has ever successfully accomplished.

As he flailed, he staggered around the yard until his foot went into the hole where the fox henchman had emerged, twisting his ankle. He fell and crashed against the hutch knocking himself out.

The others were reviving Felix, who was badly hurt but would recover.

M herself arrived along with another mouse that Felix did not know. They went over to Felix, who was sitting up and looking a bit better.

"Well done Felix. Now, all we need is to find Billie-the-Kid. Any ideas?"

"We'll have to ask Mr Floppy when he comes round."

Sydnee clipped a special collar onto Mr Floppy that would let A.I.S. know if he left the rabbit run again. It was designed so that it could not be removed without the code.

There was a call of warning and suddenly everyone scampered for cover. The little girl was coming. Felix was helped out of sight, but Mr Floppy could not be moved. He was just coming round.

"Hello, Mr Floppy. Oh, are you hurt?"

The girl hurried to her little bunny rabbit and picked it up gently.

"Oh, you've got a new collar; with flashing lights on it. I can't take it off. Oh well, at least it's pretty."

She stroked the rabbit which looked as though it was feeling a lot better now.

Chapter 20

The End ... Third time lucky?

As soon as the little girl had gone the A.I.S. agents returned and started to question Mr Floppy.

"So, Mr Floppy, also known as The Wilder Moor Beast."

The rabbit tried to look mean, but only managed to look as if it had indigestion.

"What kind of name is that to give yourself? Wilder Moor Beast, indeed," M said.

"Well, I could hardly sign the note Mr Floppy could I?"

"I suppose not. Anyway, where's the kid?" M demanded.

"I'm not telling you and you won't get it out of me. Hand over the million leaves, and take off this stupid collar, then you'll get the kid back. Not before. I need that money to escape from this stupid run and get my own place on a tropical island. This girl is pathetic. Calls me her smoochy-woochy-bunny-wabbit! I want to be sick every time she picks me up."

"You're in no position to bargain. That collar is not coming off under any circumstances, and as for giving you a million leaves, well, you can forget it."

"Well say goodbye to Billie-the-Kid then, 'cause you'll never see her alive again."

In the distance, they heard the little girl cry out, "Oh wow, a baby goat!"

Mr Floppy put his head in his hands.

"Never see her alive again eh?" M said. She nodded to the other mouse, "This is a job for you I think."

The mouse scurried away in the direction of the girl.

"Who's she then?" asked Felix.

"Human-animal relations," was M's cryptic reply.

"What's her name?"

"Nobody knows. She prefers to remain anony-mouse."

Chapter 21

The End ... Oh, come on, really? Is it? Or are you just saying that?

After a short while, the mouse returned leading Billie-the-Kid safe and sound.

"How did you manage to smooth it over with the little girl, anonymouse?" asked M.

"It's just a natural talent I have. No point explaining it, you couldn't begin to understand."

"Fair enough," said Felix, "just glad we got Billie back alright. There's still one more thing that's bothering me."

"What's that?" asked M.

"What happened to my back-up?"

"Oh yes; Eric the Red was supposed to be watching over you, from the trees, wasn't he?"

"He was; but when I got into trouble, he was nowhere to be seen. He could have warned me about the snake ambushing me, and I wouldn't look like I just went nine rounds with a gorilla."

"It's not like Eric to abandon anyone in difficulties, is it?"

"No, my thoughts exactly. I'm just wondering if he's in some sort of trouble himself."

However, before anyone could worry anymore about what had happened to Eric the Red, a bushy tail emerged from the old oak tree stump across the field. Eric was dragging something heavy, backwards towards the farm house. They couldn't see what it was because his big bushy red tail was in the way.

Billie-the-Kid was unhurt. At least Mr Floppy has taken good care of her. He had even bought her a giraffe onesie, and a snuggly blanket when she had been sad on the first day of her captivity. The General would be pleased to get her back safe.

Finally, Eric the Red arrived, dragging his heavy package which turned out to be none other than Swifty the tortoise.

"Swifty! We meet again!" Felix was jubilant, temporarily forgetting his cuts and bruises.

"Well done Eric!"

"What happened to you?" asked Eric as he took in Felix's battered appearance. "Last time I looked you had the situation under control."

"Oh, nothing, just it turns out Mr Floppy had some pretty nasty henchmen who gave me a good going over. But Glenn and Bill flew in to save the day, and Billie-the-Kid is safe and sound, and now you've even nabbed

Swifty. All in all, it's been a pretty successful day for Animal Intelligence Services."

At that, everyone cheered.

Epilogue

Oh, Rats.

On their return to H.Q. the agents of Animal Intelligence Services were jubilant. But their pleasure was short lived. Even as they drank fizzy dandelion juice, everything went dark. The lights had gone out, and so had all Sydnee's high tech equipment.

What could cause such a terrible disaster? Was it just a simple power cut? Or was it something more sinister.

They were completely in the dark.

Literally.

The End

No, really, it is this time

No point turning the page.
There's nothing more.

Oh yes.
One more thing.

The next book planned is
"Doctor Gnaw"

About the author.

Oh, alright, there is this bit.

Olli hated writing at school. He didn't like being told what to write, and he could never finish before the end of the lesson. He spent most lunch-breaks on his own in class finishing his work. Also, his hand hurt from holding a pen, and he made a ridiculous number of mistakes.

After leaving school, he went through a variety of jobs but is now more or less a full-time writer. Nobody is more surprised.

The difference was computers. No more holding a pen, and mistakes can easily be corrected. Also, he doesn't have to write what the teacher tells him, and he doesn't have to finish before the bell goes for playtime.

WIN!

About the illustrator

Amii James was chosen from a number of art students at Ilfracombe Academy who submitted work for consideration.

Amii has been artistic ever since she can remember and has always planned to pursue this through to university and eventually (hopefully) a career.

Throughout her time at Ilfracombe Academy she has been massively supported by Jeff Lawton, her art teacher, although it's often hard to tell which he enjoys more: her artwork or her attitude.

Her large, chaotic family have also been a big support, always believing in her and encouraging her to pursue what she loves

Reviews

Please don't forget to review this book.

Do a book review for school, you can use the pictures in a PowerPoint presentation to make it more interesting for the class.

Maybe get mum or dad to write a review on Amazon, but in your words. Be honest, if you don't like it, say so but always explain why.